MW01118266

SandCastle™

Baby
Australian Animals

It's a Baby
Flying Fox!

Katherine Hengel

Consulting Editor, Diane Craig, M.A./Reading Specialist

ABDO
Publishing Company

Published by ABDO Publishing Company, 8000 West 78th Street, Edina, Minnesota 55439.

Copyright © 2010 by Abdo Consulting Group, Inc. International copyrights reserved in all countries.

No part of this book may be reproduced in any form without written permission from the publisher. SandCastle™ is a trademark and logo of ABDO Publishing Company.

Printed in the United States.

Editor: Liz Salzmann
Content Developer: Nancy Tuminelly
Cover and Interior Design and Production: Kelly Doudna, Mighty Media
Photo Credits: Digital Vision, Getty Images (WIN-Initiative), iStockphoto.com (candicelo, Hanis), JupiterImages Corporation, Peter Arnold Inc. (Biosphoto/Allofs Theo, WILDLIFE), Shutterstock

Library of Congress Cataloging-in-Publication Data

Hengel, Katherine.
  It's a baby flying fox! / Katherine Hengel.
    p. cm. -- (Baby Australian animals)
  ISBN 978-1-60453-575-4
  1. Flying foxes--Infancy--Australia--Juvenile literature. I. Title.

  QL737.C575H46 2010
  599.4'9--dc22
                              2008055074

SandCastle™ Level: Transitional

SandCastle™ books are created by a team of professional educators, reading specialists, and content developers around five essential components—phonemic awareness, phonics, vocabulary, text comprehension, and fluency—to assist young readers as they develop reading skills and strategies and increase their general knowledge. All books are written, reviewed, and leveled for guided reading, early reading intervention, and Accelerated Reader® programs for use in shared, guided, and independent reading and writing activities to support a balanced approach to literacy instruction. The SandCastle™ series has four levels that correspond to early literacy development. The levels are provided to help teachers and parents select appropriate books for young readers.

Emerging Readers
(no flags)

Beginning Readers
(1 flag)

Transitional Readers
(2 flags)

Fluent Readers
(3 flags)

SandCastle™ would like to hear from you. Please send us your comments and suggestions.
sandcastle@abdopublishing.com

Vital Statistics

for the Flying Fox

BABY NAME
pup

NUMBER IN LITTER
1

WEIGHT AT BIRTH
2¾ ounces (80 g)

AGE OF INDEPENDENCE
1½ years

ADULT WEIGHT
1¼ to 2¼ pounds (600 to 1,000 g)

LIFE EXPECTANCY
3 to 15 years

Female flying foxes give **birth** in trees. They live in **colonies** with many other flying foxes.

Flying foxes are also called fruit bats.

Female flying foxes have one pup at a time. The pups cannot fly, so the mothers carry them.

When a mother flies to find food, her pup **clings** to her fur.

During the day, the mother flying fox **wraps** her pup in her wings. This **protects** the pup and keeps it warm.

Flying foxes are **nocturnal**. They rest during the day and look for food at night.

9

Flying foxes eat fruit, **nectar**, and **pollen**. The pollen sticks to their fur and they lick it off!

Flying foxes have long tongues. This helps them get **nectar** from deep inside flowers.

One of their favorite foods is the **eucalyptus** flower.

Carpet pythons, sea eagles, and crocodiles **prey** on flying foxes.

Flying foxes hang upside down because they have weak legs. It is hard for them to stand up.

Young flying foxes practice flying near their **colonies**. After about three months they can find food on their own.

Flying foxes use sight and smell to find food.

Flying foxes sometimes fly far from their **colonies** to find food. They can fly up to 60 miles (100 km) in one night.

Flying foxes can fly 15 to 25 miles per hour (25 to 40 kph).

Fun Fact

About the Flying Fox

A flying fox can have a **wingspan** of 6 feet (2 m). That's wider than most men are tall!

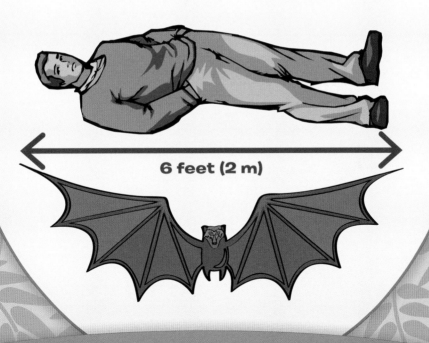

6 feet (2 m)

Glossary

birth – when a person or animal is born.

cling – to hold on tightly.

colony – a group of animals or plants that live or grow together.

eucalyptus – an Australian tree that is grown for its oil and wood.

female – being of the sex that can produce eggs or give birth. Mothers are female.

nectar – a sweet liquid found in flowers.

nocturnal – most active at night.

pollen – the fine powder found in flowers.

prey – to hunt or catch an animal for food.

protect – to guard someone or something from harm or danger.

wingspan – the distance from one wing tip to the other when the wings are fully spread.

To see a complete list of SandCastle™ books and other nonfiction titles from ABDO Publishing Company, visit **www.abdopublishing.com**.

8000 West 78th Street, Edina, MN 55439

800-800-1312 • 952-831-1632 fax